Katie AND THE
SPANISH PRINCESS

JAMES MAYHEW

ORCHARD

For a real princess
Vanessa Aduke Olusanya Pearce
(who once longed for a dress like this)
and her family
Joshua and Chloë
with love

Thanks to my splendid designer, Clare Mills, and,
as ever, to my indispensable editor, Liz Johnson.
Thanks also to Charlie Mills for the Katie pirate picture on Page 32.

ORCHARD BOOKS
Carmelite House, 50 Victoria Embankment, London EC4Y 0DZ

ISBN 978 1 40833 242 9

First published in 2006 by Orchard Books
First published in paperback in 2006
This edition published in 2015

Text and illustrations © James Mayhew 2006/2015
The rights of James Mayhew to be identified as the author and
illustrator of this work have been asserted by him in accordance
with the Copyright, Designs and Patents Act, 1988.
A CIP catalogue record for this book is available from the British Library.

2 4 6 8 10 9 7 5 3 1

Printed in China

FSC
www.fsc.org

MIX
Paper from
responsible sources
FSC® C104740

Orchard Books is an imprint of Hachette Children's Group, part of
The Watts Publishing Group Limited, an Hachette UK company.
www.hachette.co.uk

www.jamesmayhew.co.uk

Acknowledgements
Portrait of the Infanta Margarita (1651-73) Aged Five, 1656 (oil on canvas), Velazquez, Diego Rodriguez de Silva y
(1599-1660) / Kunsthistorisches Museum, Vienna, Austria / Bridgeman Images. *Manuel Osorio Manrique from Zuniga*,
by Francisco de Goya (1746-1828), oil on canvas, 1790 / De Agostini Picture Library / Bridgeman Images. *The Parasol*,
1777 (oil on canvas), Goya y Lucientes, Francisco Jose de (1746-1828) / Prado, Madrid, Spain / Bridgeman Images.
A Peasant Boy Leaning on a Sill, 1670-80 (oil on canvas), Murillo, Bartolome Esteban (1618-82) / National Gallery,
London, UK / Bridgeman Images. *Philip IV (1605-65) of Spain in Brown and Silver*, c.1631-2 (oil on canvas), Velazquez,
Diego Rodriguez de Silva y (1599-1660) / National Gallery, London, UK / Bridgeman Images.

TOMORROW WAS KATIE'S BIRTHDAY and Grandma was
making a princess costume for her fancy-dress party.
But the costume didn't look quite right . . .
"We need to see some princess pictures," said Grandma.
"Let's go to the gallery."

At the gallery, Katie and Grandma found a picture called
Portrait of the Infanta Margarita by Diego Velázquez.
"She must be a princess," said Katie. "Look at her dress!"

"It doesn't look very comfy," said Grandma, sitting down.
"Now, I'll just have a quick snooze while you look around."
"It might not be a comfy dress," sighed Katie, "but it *is* beautiful."

"Do you really think so?" said a voice.
Katie looked around, but there was
no one there except Grandma
and she was sound asleep.

"Did you say something?"
Katie asked Margarita.
"Yes, but I'm not really supposed
to speak," whispered the princess.
"Quickly, come inside!"

And she helped Katie into the picture.

"Shall we play together?" asked Margarita.
"I'm fed up with being quiet and good, and
behaving like a princess."
"Let's play dressing up," said Katie. "I'll be
a princess and you can be a . . . a . . . "
"I can be you!" cried Margarita.
"We'll swap clothes."

They quickly changed clothes.

"How do I look?" asked Katie.

"Like a princess!" giggled Margarita. "And now you must behave like one."

"Easy," laughed Katie. "And you have to behave like me!"

"At last, I'm free!" shouted Margarita, jumping into the gallery.
Katie found it hard to keep up in the enormous dress.
"Wait for me!" she called.

Margarita waited for Katie to catch up. "Let's look
at the pictures," she said. "Which is your favourite?"
"That one," said Katie, pointing to a picture called *Don Manuel
Osorio de Zuniga* by Francisco Goya. "Look at all his pets!"

Suddenly, a bird swooped out of the picture and snatched the jewel from the beautiful dress.
"A magpie!" said Katie.

"His name is Pluma," said the little boy, tearfully. "He loves shiny things. Oh, where has he gone?"
"Don't worry, Manuel," said Margarita. "We'll catch him."

"This dress is impossible to run in!" said Katie,
as they chased Pluma. But they couldn't catch him
and he flew inside another painting.

It was called *The Parasol* by Francisco Goya.
"Come on," said Margarita. "Let's go inside."
And they clambered through the frame.

"Greetings, Your Majesty!" said a young couple
with a dog. They thought Katie was the real princess!
"Look, there's Pluma," said Margarita. "He's up in that tree."
"How are we going to catch him?" asked Katie.
"You mustn't climb up in that dress," said
the young man. "You'll spoil it."
"Send your servant instead," said the lady,
pointing at Margarita.

Margarita climbed up the tree. She was just about
to catch the bird when the dog started
barking. Pluma flew off into the gallery.
"Come on, Margarita!" said Katie. "Follow that bird!"
"What a strange princess," said the lady.

There was no sign of Pluma in the gallery, but they could hear someone laughing. It was a scruffy little boy in a painting called *A Peasant Boy Leaning on a Sill* by Bartolomé Murillo.

"Are you looking for a bird?" asked the boy. "It flew in here."

So Margarita and Katie squeezed through the small frame.

They found themselves in the ruins of an
old house. Pluma was perched out of reach
on a high windowsill.
"I've got an idea," whispered the boy.
He broke up a piece of bread and scattered
the crumbs. "It's the last of my food,
so I hope it works."

Pluma spotted the bread and flew down.
In a flash, the boy caught the bird and handed
the jewel back to Katie.
"Thank you," said Katie. "It was kind of you to use
your bread to catch Pluma."
The boy bowed and said, "You're welcome, Your Majesty."

"Manuel will be worried about Pluma," said Margarita,
taking the bird. "We should go."

"That poor boy must be very hungry," said Katie,
waving goodbye.

"Yes," said Margarita. "We always have plenty of food,
so I suppose I'm lucky being a princess, really."

They walked back to Pluma's picture,
where Manuel was waiting anxiously.

"You found him!" he said, gently stroking Pluma.
"Make sure you hold onto his ribbon," said Katie.
"I will," said Manuel. "Thank you!"

Suddenly they heard a loud voice.
"Margarita! Where are you?"
"Oh, it's Papa!" said Margarita.
Katie saw a tall man in a painting
called *Philip IV of Spain in Brown
and Silver* by Diego Velázquez.
"Goodness me!" she gasped.
"A real king!"

"I'm here, Papa," said Margarita.

"Heavens, what are you wearing?" said the king.

"And who is this other little princess?"

"This is my friend, Katie," said Margarita.

"We swapped clothes so she could be a princess for the day!"

"And did you enjoy being a princess?" asked the king.
"Well," said Katie, "it's quite hard to have fun in such
fancy clothes."
"It certainly is," laughed the king. "Now change back,
you two, before anyone sees you!"

They stepped into Margarita's picture
and changed back into their own clothes.
"It was fun to be you for a while," said
Margarita. "But it's good to be me again."

Katie laughed. "Thanks for letting
me be a princess. Goodbye!"
"*Adios*, my friend," said Margarita.

Katie gently woke Grandma.

"Come on," said Grandma. "Let's go and have some lemonade."

"And a slice of cake!" said Katie.

Katie chose a large slice of chocolate cake. She was just about to eat it when she thought of something . . .
"Back in a minute, Grandma!" said Katie.

She went back to the picture of the scruffy boy. He was surprised to see that Katie wasn't really a princess.
"You must be hungry," said Katie. "Have my cake."
"You're very kind," he said. "*Gracias*!"

Katie ran back and finished her lemonade.

"Come on," said Grandma. "Let's go home and make that princess costume."

"Thanks, Grandma," said Katie. "But I don't think I want to be a princess any more . . . I want to be a pirate, instead!"

Get creative with Katie!

The famous artist Diego Velázquez was such a good artist he worked for the King of Spain, painting portraits of the Royal Family, including Princess Margarita.

Have you ever been to a fancy dress party? It can be lots of fun to dress up. Maybe you can think of something you'd like to be. Why not have a go at designing a costume for yourself?

You don't have to design a dress for a princess, though. There are lots of other costumes you can create...

Katie has drawn a picture of her favourite costume – a pirate! Have Fun!

Love Katie x